Is Todd Headed for Trouble?

Todd sighed. "OK. So I cheated. Big deal."

"It is a big deal. Especially if you get caught," Elizabeth said.

Todd looked scared. "You're not going to tell on me, are you?"

"No," Elizabeth said slowly. "But what if Mrs. Otis catches you?"

Todd laughed. "I'm not going to get caught. Cheating is easy."

Bantam Books in the SWEET VALLEY KIDS series

SWEET VALLEY KIDS

ELIZABETH
THE
TATTLETALE

Written by
Molly Mia Stewart

Created by
FRANCINE PASCAL

Illustrated by
Ying-Hwa Hu

BANTAM BOOKS
NEW YORK•TORONTO•LONDON•SYDNEY•AUCKLAND

To Samuel Allen Forman

RL 2, 005-008

ELIZABETH THE TATTLETALE
A Bantam Book / March 1994

*Sweet Valley High® and Sweet Valley Kids are
trademarks of Francine Pascal*

Conceived by Francine Pascal

*Produced by Daniel Weiss Associates, Inc.
33 West 17th Street
New York, NY 10011*

Cover art by Susan Tang

ISBN: 0-553-48110-X

Published simultaneously in the United States and Canada

*Bantam Books are published by Bantam Books, a division of Bantam
Doubleday Dell Publishing Group, Inc. Its trademark, consisting of the
words "Bantam Books" and the portrayal of a rooster, is Registered in
U.S. Patent and Trademark Office and in other countries. Marca
Registrada. Bantam Books, 1540 Broadway, New York, New York 10036.*

PRINTED IN THE UNITED STATES OF AMERICA

CWO   0 9 8 7 6 5 4 3 2 1

CHAPTER 1

Fraction Champs

Elizabeth Wakefield pinched her nose shut. "Fractions stink," she said, making a face. "They're hard."

Jessica Wakefield, Elizabeth's twin sister, laughed. "But we don't stink at figuring them out."

Mrs. Otis stopped next to Jessica's and Elizabeth's desks. Mrs. Otis was the twins' second-grade teacher. She had dark hair and wore glasses. The twins both thought she was an outstanding teacher.

"We're going to get every problem

right on tomorrow's test," Elizabeth told Mrs. Otis. "We've been studying."

Jessica raised her fists above her head. "We'll be fraction champs."

Mrs. Otis smiled. "All right, champs. Here's a review sheet for the test. It should be a snap for you." She handed each of the twins a page covered with problems.

Jessica and Elizabeth glanced at their review sheets.

"P.U.!" they both said at exactly the same time. Then they both giggled.

Jessica and Elizabeth often did the same thing at the same time. That's because they were identical twins. They looked exactly alike. Each girl had blue-green eyes and long blond hair with bangs. When they wore matching outfits, even their best friends had a hard time telling them apart. It helped a lot that they wore name bracelets.

Jessica and Elizabeth looked like two peas in a pod, but their personalities were very different. Elizabeth loved to read and make up stories, and she enjoyed her classes at school. She played for the Sweet Valley Soccer League and didn't mind diving into the mud to stop a ball. Green was her favorite color.

Jessica was the opposite. Her favorite part of school was recess and talking with friends. She liked to wear pretty clothes and was always careful to keep them clean. That's why she preferred to play games like hopscotch and jump rope. She thought pink was the best color.

In spite of their differences, Elizabeth and Jessica were best friends. They sat next to each other at school, they shared a bedroom, and they loved to share secrets. No matter what, they knew they would be best friends forever.

Elizabeth did the problems on her review sheet as fast as she could. Jessica finished a minute later. The girls took their sheets up to Mrs. Otis's desk together.

Mrs. Otis graded their work while they waited. "You got every problem right, Elizabeth. Jessica, you have a perfect paper, too. Identical one hundred percents for identical twins."

Elizabeth smiled at Jessica. She knew they were both ready for the big test.

"You may read your library books until everyone else finishes," Mrs. Otis told them.

Elizabeth ran to her cubby and got

out *Bunnies at the Beach*. It was the latest book by Angela Daley, Elizabeth's favorite author. The school library had just gotten it, and Elizabeth was the first one to check it out. She loved all of Ms. Daley's books, especially since the author had visited Mrs. Otis's class and read a story Elizabeth had written.

Elizabeth carried the book back to her desk. She tucked her feet under her and started reading. When she got to the end of the first chapter, Elizabeth glanced around the room. Most of her classmates had finished their review sheets and were now reading quietly. Most, except for Jessica, who was passing notes with her friends Lila Fowler and Ellen Riteman.

Elizabeth didn't mind that some people were taking longer to finish. It meant she could spend more time reading. Elizabeth had just gotten to the middle of the second chapter in her book when she heard Mrs. Otis call her name.

"Elizabeth, would you please help Todd finish his review sheet? Ken is absent today; otherwise, I'd ask him." Ken Matthews sat next to Todd and understood fractions well. But Todd wasn't having an easy time of it. Especially not on his own.

Elizabeth put down her book and went to sit at Ken's desk. Ken and Todd sat right behind her and Jessica. Todd had brown hair and brown eyes. He played on the soccer team with Elizabeth. Even though Todd was a boy, he was one of Elizabeth's best friends.

"I hate fractions." Todd sounded

grumpy. "And fractions hate me."

"Oh, come on, Todd. They're not so bad. You always liked math before. Let's start with the first problem," Elizabeth said. "Once you have the easy ones right, the others won't be hard."

"If you say so," Todd agreed reluctantly.

"I say so." One by one, Elizabeth helped Todd figure out the problems for himself. She was careful not to tell him the answers.

"Thanks," Todd said when he was ready to turn in his review sheet. "Maybe you could help me tomorrow, too."

Elizabeth laughed. "Sorry, Todd. Nobody can help you during a test."

"I guess not," Todd said. "But it would be great if someone could."

CHAPTER 2

Special Delivery

"Meet me by the big wall," Lila whispered to Jessica as the class lined up to go out for recess. "And come alone," she added as Elizabeth walked toward them.

"Why?" Jessica asked. She didn't like the big wall. It was at the end of the playground, far from the school building. There was something creepy about it.

"I have a secret," Lila said. "I told Ellen to be there."

"OK," Jessica agreed. She loved secrets, and the big wall was the perfect place to tell one because hardly a soul went near it.

When they all got outside, Jessica told Elizabeth she'd catch up with her later. She watched as her sister ran toward the jungle gym. Todd, Kisho Murasaki, and Amy Sutton were already climbing the lower bars.

Jessica ran all the way to the end of the playground. Lila and Ellen had beat her to the wall.

"So what's the big secret?" Jessica asked Lila.

"I got something." Lila gave the other girls a mysterious smile. "I bet you can't guess what it is."

"Bad breath?" Jessica guessed.

Ellen giggled.

"Very funny." Lila looked disgusted. "You're not even close."

"OK, I give up," Jessica said.

"What is it?" Ellen asked.

Lila gave Jessica a dirty look. For a second, Jessica was afraid she wasn't going to tell them the secret. But Lila couldn't keep the news to herself. "I got the jokes we sent away for. The package was waiting for me when I got home yesterday."

"Cool," Ellen said.

"Wow," Jessica breathed. "I almost forgot about them."

About two months earlier, Lila had gotten a practical jokes catalog in the mail. Jessica and Ellen had been at her house the day it arrived. The three of them had spent the afternoon looking though the catalog, and after a lot of arguing, they ordered two jokes.

"I can't wait to open the package,"

11

Ellen said. "Can we come to your house after school?"

Lila rolled her eyes at Ellen. "I opened the package yesterday, silly," she said.

"That's not fair. You should have waited for us," Ellen said. "We put in almost as much money as you did."

"Money for what?" a voice demanded.

Jessica, Ellen, and Lila spun around. The voice belonged to Caroline Pearce. The other girls exchanged looks. None of them trusted Caroline. She was in their class and everyone knew she was a big tattletale. Jessica, Ellen, and Lila didn't want her to know about their jokes. She would tell and ruin everything.

"It's a secret," Ellen told Caroline.

"I can keep a secret," Caroline said.

Lila laughed. "No, you can't! Everyone knows that."

"We're not going to tell you anything," Jessica told Caroline. "So why don't you go away?"

Caroline put her hands on her hips. "You guys don't own this playground. I can stand here if I want to."

"Fine," Jessica said. "You stay here. We'll leave."

Jessica, Ellen, and Lila ran toward the other side of the playground. There were a lot of kids around. Now they would have to be extra careful no one overheard them.

The girls put their heads together. Jessica put one arm around Lila's shoulders and one arm around Ellen's shoulders. Lila and Ellen closed the circle. They looked like football players in a huddle.

"I'm still mad at you for opening our package," Ellen whispered.

"It's my package, too," Lila whispered. "It came to *my* house and had *my* name on it. Besides, I couldn't wait." Lila giggled. "One of the jokes is really gross!"

"Maybe you could bring them to school tomorrow," Jessica suggested.

"No," Lila said. "If Mrs. Otis finds out, she'll take them away. But maybe I'll bring one in."

Lila was being bossy, as usual. Jessica didn't like that. But she was too excited to get mad at Lila.

"Who should we play our first joke on?" Jessica asked.

"Mrs. Armstrong," Lila suggested with a sly smile. Mrs. Armstrong was the principal of Sweet Valley Elementary School.

Jessica giggled. "No! We'd get in too much trouble. I think we should pick a kid."

"How about Elizabeth?" Lila suggested.

"No way!" Jessica said, shaking her head.

Ellen shook her head, too. "Elizabeth would just laugh. I want to pick someone who's going to get really angry or get all embarrassed and turn purple."

"How about Andy Franklin?" Jessica suggested. "He hates to be teased." Andy was one of the smartest kids in Mrs. Otis's class. He read lots of fat books about science.

"Good idea," Ellen said.

"Perfect," Lila said.

The girls broke their huddle. Caroline was standing right next to them.

"Oh, no," Ellen groaned.

"Told you this was a free playground. And now I know you're going to do something to Andy," Caroline said, wagging a finger at them. "You'd better tell me what it is."

"What should we do?" Jessica whispered to the others.

Ellen shrugged. "Can she tell on us if she doesn't know what we're doing?"

"Caroline already knows we're planning *something*," Lila whispered back. "Maybe if we tell her exactly what, she'll think she's in on it and keep the secret."

"It's worth a try, I guess," Ellen said.

"So what are you going to do to Andy?" Caroline repeated.

"Do you promise not to tell?" Jessica asked her.

"Cross my heart," Caroline said eagerly.

Jessica cupped her hand around Caroline's ear and whispered their secret plan. Jessica hoped Caroline wouldn't tell.

CHAPTER 3

The Big Test

"Yuck," Amy said the next morning. The bell signaling the end of morning recess had just rung, and everyone had to go back to class. "We have to take the fractions test now."

"I can't wait for it to be over," Elizabeth said. She was good at fractions, but thinking about the test gave Elizabeth butterflies in her stomach.

The two girls lined up to go inside.

Todd was standing in front of Amy and Elizabeth. He had been playing dodgeball. His face was all red, and his hair was damp with sweat.

"Are you nervous about the test?" Elizabeth asked him.

"A little," Todd admitted. "But I bet I'll do fine."

"I guess you studied last night, then?" Elizabeth said.

"Well, um . . ." Todd muttered. "You could say that. I did study the best way to do well."

Elizabeth frowned. "I don't understand."

"Don't worry about it. It's a secret," Todd said. He looked up and saw Ken getting on line. Todd patted Elizabeth's shoulder. "See you later. Good luck on the test." He ran toward the back of the line and whispered something in Ken's ear.

Elizabeth wondered what Todd's secret was. She wondered why he couldn't tell it to her, but he could tell it to Ken. Elizabeth didn't have much time to think about the answer, though. Mrs. Otis came out of the building and led the class inside. As soon as they got settled, she passed out the fractions test.

"You may begin," Mrs. Otis told the class. "Remember to keep your eyes on your own paper."

Jessica looked at the test. "P.U.," she whispered.

Elizabeth giggled. "Good luck," she told her sister. She took a deep breath and went to work.

A few minutes later, Elizabeth finished problem number five. *Halfway done,* she told herself. *It's not that hard.* Just then, out of the corner of her eye, Elizabeth saw a flash of white. She glanced behind her. Nothing. Everyone was hard at work.

21

Elizabeth did three more problems. Then she saw it again. Elizabeth was almost positive Ken had just passed Todd a note.

This time Elizabeth turned all the way around and stared at Ken and Todd. But the boys didn't look back at her. Their heads were bent low over their papers as they worked. They didn't seem to be doing anything wrong. Elizabeth thought she had imagined the flash of white. Then she noticed that one of Todd's hands was under his desk. She saw his eyes dart down. Then he wrote an answer to one of the problems.

Elizabeth turned back around. She tried to finish the last two problems on the test, but she had a hard time concentrating. She had just seen Todd cheating. She was almost one hundred percent sure of it.

By the time the lunch bell rang, Elizabeth felt as if she were going to burst. "I have to tell you a secret," she whispered to Jessica.

"Really!" Jessica said, looking curious. "What is it?"

Elizabeth led Jessica to a quiet corner in the lunchroom. "You have to promise not to tell."

"I promise," Jessica said.

"Give me the special promise sign," Elizabeth insisted. "Cross your heart and snap your fingers. That way I know you won't tell."

Jessica made the sign. "I promise not to tell anyone your secret. Now will you tell it to *me*?"

Elizabeth looked around to be sure no one was listening. Then she leaned in close to Jessica. "Todd cheated on the test," she whispered.

"I saw Ken pass him the answers."

Jessica's eyes widened. "Are you sure?"

Elizabeth nodded.

"Are you going to tell Mrs. Otis?" Jessica asked.

"I don't know," Elizabeth said. "I don't want to be a tattletale."

"Then what are you going to do?" Jessica asked.

"I guess I'll talk to Todd," Elizabeth said.

"That's a good idea," Jessica agreed. "What will you tell him?"

Elizabeth sighed. "Ask me later. I'll think of something by then."

As they broke apart to join their friends for lunch, they saw Caroline a few feet away. She was tying her shoe. . . .

CHAPTER 4

A Practical Joke

Jessica thought she had the best seat in Mrs. Otis's class. She sat between her two best friends, Elizabeth and Lila. Ellen sat just on the other side of Lila. When one of her friends needed to tell her something, it was easy to pass notes or whisper to her.

"It's almost time," Lila whispered to Jessica on Friday.

"I'm ready," Jessica whispered back. "Don't worry."

Ellen leaned over Lila's desk. "Where is it?" she asked.

"Shh!" Jessica said. "I put it in my desk."

"Be careful no one sees you take it out," Lila whispered.

"I will!" Jessica said loudly.

Caroline turned around and gave Jessica an angry look. Jessica smiled sweetly at her.

The only problem with Jessica's desk was that Caroline sat right in front of her. Caroline never wanted to miss one word Mrs. Otis said. She never whispered and didn't like those who did. So she was always turning around to tell Jessica and her friends to be quiet.

Mrs. Otis was handing back the fractions test from the day before. She put the papers facedown on each student's desk.

Jessica turned her paper over and smiled. "I got an A. What did you get, Liz?"

"B," Elizabeth told her. "I made stupid mistakes on the last problems."

Elizabeth motioned for Jessica to come closer.

Jessica leaned toward her sister.

"Can you see Ken's grade?" Elizabeth whispered. Ken sat right behind Elizabeth.

Jessica leaned back. She could see Ken's paper perfectly. "He got a B," she whispered to Elizabeth.

"I saw Todd's paper," Elizabeth whispered back. "He got a B, too. Which problems did Ken miss?"

"Two and nine," Jessica whispered.

"Same as Todd," Elizabeth whispered back. "Now I know I wasn't seeing things yesterday. They were cheating."

Lila tapped Jessica on the shoulder. "Now," she whispered when Jessica turned around.

"Go on!" Ellen added.

"Give me a minute," Jessica whispered back. She was getting dizzy. Keeping two secrets straight was confusing.

Jessica turned back to Elizabeth. "I think you'd better talk to Todd soon."

Elizabeth was about to say something else, but Jessica held up her hand. "Tell me later. I have to sharpen my pencil."

Jessica ignored the funny look Elizabeth gave her. She reached into her desk with her left hand and slid something into her pocket. In her right hand, Jessica picked up her pencil.

Jessica walked to the front of the room. As she passed Andy's desk in the first row, she pulled out what was in her pocket and bent down to drop it on the floor. Then Jessica hurried toward the pencil sharpener. While she was sharpening her pencil, Jessica glanced back toward her seat.

Ellen was covering her mouth. Lila was biting her lip. They were both trying hard not to giggle. So was Jessica. They were waiting for Andy to notice what was next to him.

"Any second," Lila mouthed silently.

But Andy wasn't the first to notice. Winston Egbert, the class clown, was.

"Eew! It's going to smell real bad in a few seconds, Mrs. Otis!" he yelled. "Look what Andy did. Get me away!"

Everyone got out of his or her seat and crowded to the front. They looked at Andy and then down at the floor around his desk.

"Yuck!" several kids shouted.

"Gross!" others yelled.

"I didn't do anything," Andy said. He

stood on his chair. "Honest."

Then Caroline pushed her way through the cluster of kids. "Mrs. Otis!" she shouted. "Jessica and Lila and Ellen are playing a gross joke on Andy. It's fake vomit!" Caroline looked up at Andy. "Don't worry. You can come down. It's just plastic."

Ellen, Lila, and Jessica rolled their eyes. The other kids in the class groaned. Caroline was being a tattletale, and nobody liked a tattletale.

"Grow up," Andy told Caroline. "It's a good joke." He smiled at Jessica, Lila, and Ellen.

Jessica was glad Andy thought their joke was funny. She looked over at Mrs. Otis and saw that the teacher was smiling, too.

CHAPTER 5

Cheating Is Easy

Elizabeth stood in the lunchroom doorway and glanced around. Jessica and most of the other girls in Mrs. Otis's class were sitting at one long table. Elizabeth saw an empty seat next to her sister. She knew Jessica was saving it for her.

Todd was sitting by himself, unwrapping a sandwich. Ken and Winston were standing near the end of the hot-lunch line. Winston and Ken always ate with Todd. But if Elizabeth hurried, she could talk to him for a few minutes before the other boys came over.

Elizabeth walked up to Todd's table and sat down. "Hi!"

"Hi," Todd said.

Elizabeth unwrapped her sandwich and took a little bite. She wasn't sure where to begin. Finally she asked, "What did you get on the fractions test?"

"B," Todd said.

"I'm surprised you didn't get an A," Elizabeth said.

Todd put down his carton of milk and gave Elizabeth a funny look. "How come? You know I'm not good at fractions."

Elizabeth saw that Ken and Winston were already getting their mini-pizzas. "I thought you'd get an A because you got help."

"What are you talking about?" Todd asked innocently.

"You know what I mean. You cheated," Elizabeth said.

Todd's face turned bright red. "I did not!"

"Then what was Ken passing you during the test?" Elizabeth asked.

"He didn't pass me anything," Todd said.

"He did too," Elizabeth insisted. "I saw it. It was a white piece of paper."

Todd sighed. "OK. So I cheated. Big deal."

"It is a big deal. Especially if you get caught," Elizabeth said.

Todd looked scared. "You're not going to tell on me, are you?"

"No," Elizabeth said slowly. "But what if Mrs. Otis catches you?"

Todd laughed. "Mrs. Otis won't catch me. She already gave the tests back."

"Still . . ." Elizabeth said.

"I'm not going to get caught," Todd told her. "Cheating is easy. I wish I had tried it before the *last* math test."

Elizabeth shook her head. "I can't believe Ken helped you. He should know better, too."

"Why?" Todd asked. "Ken's not a goody two-shoes—like some people."

Elizabeth stood up. "I am not a goody two-shoes, and you know it."

"Where are you going?" Todd asked.

"I have to study for the spelling quiz," Elizabeth said. She was a good speller because she always studied.

"I know a way you can get all the words right without studying," Todd said.

"How?" Elizabeth asked.

"I'll show you." Todd pulled a tiny slip of paper out of his pocket and handed it to Elizabeth. He had printed

all the spelling words on the paper. The words were so small, Elizabeth had to squint to see them. Still, they were all there.

"If Mrs. Otis comes by, I'm going to eat it," Todd said. "That way there won't be any evidence."

Elizabeth handed the paper back to Todd. "But you don't need to cheat in spelling, Todd. You're a good speller."

Todd shrugged. "It's easier this way. I didn't have to study at all."

"It's wrong," Elizabeth said.

"Goody two-shoes," Todd said.

Elizabeth glared at Todd and stomped away just as Winston and Ken slipped into seats at the table.

By the time the spelling quiz started that afternoon, Elizabeth had developed another case of butterflies. She wasn't nervous about how she would do on the quiz. Elizabeth was afraid Mrs. Otis would catch Todd. If that happened, he would be in big trouble.

But Todd only looked at his cheat sheet when Mrs. Otis was facing the other way. She didn't notice a thing. Mrs. Otis graded the quizzes and passed them back right away.

"What did you get?" Todd asked Elizabeth.

"An eighty-five," Elizabeth told him.

Todd smirked. "I got a hundred!"

Elizabeth wasn't impressed. She knew why Todd's grade was better than hers. And she didn't like it one bit.

CHAPTER 6

The Prize

Jessica was watching the big clock that hung over the classroom door. In seven minutes, another week of school would be over. Jessica loved Friday afternoons. She had two whole days without school to look forward to. And this was not an ordinary Friday. It was special because Lila and Ellen were both coming over after school. Jessica and her friends were going to plan their next practical joke—where Caroline couldn't hear.

The minute hand on the clock seemed

to have stopped. Jessica sighed. At this rate, the weekend would never come.

Elizabeth poked Jessica.

Jessica pulled her eyes away from the clock and faced front.

Mrs. Otis was looking right at her. "Jessica Wakefield," the teacher was saying. "It is not the weekend yet. I need your attention for a few more minutes, please."

Jessica could feel her face get hot. "I'm sorry," she mumbled.

"Monday morning we are going to have a mini–spelling bee," Mrs. Otis announced.

"But we just had a spelling quiz," Jessica complained.

Mrs. Otis smiled. "I know I've been working you hard lately, but this is going to be a special spelling bee. A fun one."

"What could be fun about it?" Charlie Cashman called out. He was one of the bigger boys in the class and often bullied kids in the playground.

"The winner is going to get a prize," Mrs. Otis said.

"What kind of a prize?" Caroline asked.

"Three tickets to a professional soccer game," Mrs. Otis announced.

"Wow!" Elizabeth breathed. She turned around and smiled at Todd. Todd and Elizabeth were two of the biggest soccer fans in the class.

Eva Simpson raised her hand. "What words should we study?" she asked. Eva played on the soccer team, too. Of course, she also wanted to win the tickets.

Jessica wasn't excited about the spelling bee. She didn't like soccer, and she didn't want to go to a soccer game.

While Mrs. Otis told the class which words to study, Jessica glanced back at the clock. Only three minutes to go!

When the bell finally rang, Lila, Ellen, and the twins walked to the bus together. Jessica felt important having two guests.

"My dad is taking us to the beach tomorrow," Ellen bragged.

"Lucky!" Jessica turned to Elizabeth. "Let's get Mom and Dad to take us, too."

Elizabeth shook her head. "I want to spend all weekend studying."

"All weekend?" Ellen repeated.

"How come?" Lila asked.

"I want to win the spelling bee," Elizabeth said.

"I bet Jessica wins," Ellen said.

Jessica smiled. It was nice to hear Ellen say she was going to win. Not long ago, Jessica had represented Sweet Valley Elementary School at the district spelling bee. Some of her classmates—including Ellen—wanted Elizabeth to go in her place. They thought Jessica wasn't smart enough to win. But she had won! That made her the best second-grade speller in the entire school district.

"I'm not going to study at all," Jessica announced. As a spelling-bee champion, she felt that was her right.

"Are you sure?" Elizabeth asked. "You studied lots before the district bee. That's why you did so well."

Jessica shrugged. "I don't care if I win this time. What would I do with a bunch of soccer tickets?"

"That's easy," Elizabeth said with a grin. "Give them to me."

CHAPTER 7

Cheat Sheet

"OK, everybody," Mrs. Otis said. "Line up at the front of the room."

Elizabeth got up and ran to get in line. It was Monday, and the spelling bee was about to begin. Elizabeth was excited as she found a place between Jessica and Amy. She hadn't spent the *whole* weekend studying—but she had studied for many hours. After everyone lined up, Mrs. Otis explained the rules. She would pronounce a word for each student. The student had to say the word, spell it, then say it again. If the word was spelled correctly, the student stayed in line. If the word was spelled incorrectly, the student had to sit down and the next one in line had to spell that word.

Charlie was at the front of the line.

"The word is *secret*," Mrs. Otis told him.

"Um, *secret*," Charlie said. "S-e-k-r-e-t. *Secret*."

"Sorry, that's not right," Mrs. Otis said. "You may take your seat."

As Charlie stomped back to his seat, Elizabeth and Jessica exchanged looks. The very first person had missed his word. This was not a good way to begin. Elizabeth began to get nervous.

Soon it was Jessica's turn. Her word was *snack*. Elizabeth listened carefully as Jessica spelled. If she made a mistake, Elizabeth would have to spell *snack*. But Jessica spelled the word correctly.

"Your word is *sister*," Mrs. Otis told Elizabeth.

Elizabeth felt like laughing. What an easy word. But Elizabeth didn't want to make a stupid mistake, so she concentrated.

"*Sister*," Elizabeth said. "S-i-s-t-e-r. *Sister*."

"Good job," Mrs. Otis said.

Elizabeth beamed.

Jerry McAllister, Sandra Ferris, Kisho, and Ellen also misspelled their first words and had to sit down.

Everyone else moved closer together. Elizabeth's heart was beating faster. She was getting close to winning the tickets.

"Caroline, your word is *hamster*," Mrs. Otis said.

"Hamster." Caroline paused to think. "H-a-m-s-t-i-r. *Hamster.*"

Mrs. Otis shook her head. "Sorry."

Caroline frowned and walked toward her seat. Eva was next in line. "Can you spell *hamster*?" Mrs. Otis asked her.

Eva didn't need time to think. She spelled *hamster* without any trouble. Elizabeth could tell that Eva had studied. She seemed very sure of herself.

In the second round the words got harder, but the twins each got theirs right. By the end of the round only six kids were left: Andy, Todd, Elizabeth, Jessica, Eva, and Jim Sturbridge.

Elizabeth was standing next to Todd. Andy was on Todd's other side.

"OK, Andy," Mrs. Otis said. "Can you spell *telephone*?"

"Telephone," Andy muttered. He

sounded as if he didn't know how to spell it. If Andy missed the word, Todd would have to try. Elizabeth turned to smile at Todd, but he didn't see her. Todd was pretending to itch his nose. What he was really doing was looking at a cheat sheet. Elizabeth couldn't believe it. She spent all weekend studying and Todd was *cheating*. Elizabeth had been worried about Todd before—but now she was mad!

"Telephone," Andy said. "T-e-l-a-p-o-n-e. *Telephone*."

Mrs. Otis made a face. "Sorry, Andy, that's not right. Give it a try, Todd."

Todd itched his nose again. Then he spelled *telephone* exactly right. Elizabeth wasn't surprised.

"Great job," Mrs. Otis told Todd. "Elizabeth, your word is *sentence*."

Elizabeth stared at Mrs. Otis. Why

didn't she notice Todd was cheating?

"Elizabeth?" Mrs. Otis said.

"Sorry," Elizabeth mumbled. "Could you tell me the word again, please?"

"*Sentence,*" Mrs. Otis repeated.

"*Sentence,*" Elizabeth said, glaring at Todd. "S-e-n-t-e-n-s-e. *Sentence.*"

"I'm sorry, Elizabeth," Mrs. Otis said. "That's not right."

Jessica gave Elizabeth a funny look. Elizabeth shook her head. She knew how to spell *sentence.* She had only made a mistake because Todd had gotten her so upset.

Elizabeth sat down, feeling crabby. She didn't mind losing fair and square. But Todd was cheating. Elizabeth wished Mrs. Otis would catch him.

Jessica spelled *sentence* correctly, but Eva and Jim both missed their words. The bee was down to Jessica and Todd.

Elizabeth crossed her fingers for good luck. Maybe Jessica would win even though Todd was cheating. Maybe Mrs. Otis would give Todd a word that wasn't on his list.

"The word is *professor*," Mrs. Otis told Jessica.

Jessica took a deep breath.

"You can do it," Elizabeth said quietly. *Professor* was a hard word, but Jessica was a good speller.

"*Professor*," Jessica said carefully. "P-r-o-f-e-s-s-e-r. *Professor*."

Elizabeth's heart sank. She didn't know how to spell *professor*. But she knew Jessica had gotten the word wrong when she saw Mrs. Otis shake her head.

Todd spelled the word correctly and won the tickets.

"Sorry," Jessica whispered to Elizabeth as she slid into her seat.

"Don't be," Elizabeth whispered back. "Todd was cheating."

"What?" Jessica's eyes were wide.

"He cheated," Elizabeth said. "I saw his cheat sheet."

"You should tell Mrs. Otis," Jessica said. "He can't keep doing this."

"I will!" Elizabeth raised her hand.

"Yes, Elizabeth?" Mrs. Otis asked.

"Um—" Elizabeth said. She was stalling. She couldn't tattle on Todd. He was a cheat, but he was also her friend. "Nothing."

Mrs. Otis gave Elizabeth a funny look. Elizabeth slumped down in her seat. She passed Todd a note. It read, YOU BETTER STOP—BEFORE YOU GET CAUGHT.

Todd read the note. Then he stared hard at Elizabeth and ripped the note into tiny pieces.

CHAPTER 8

Caught

Jessica glanced at Lila and Ellen. It was Tuesday morning just before attendance. The girls watched as Caroline walked toward her cubby and opened it.

"Eieeee!" Caroline screamed, jumping back.

Lila, Ellen, and Jessica started to laugh.

"Mrs. Otis!" Caroline screamed. "There's a frog in my cubby."

Mrs. Otis went to look. "So there is. But calm down, Caroline. It's just a *plastic* frog. Someone's playing a joke on you."

Caroline was furious. "Jessica and Lila and Ellen put that icky thing in there." She stomped her foot. "They're being mean to me. Make them stop!"

"Caroline, would you please quiet down and take your seat," Mrs. Otis said.

Jessica expected to get in trouble. But Mrs. Otis didn't say anything to her, Lila, or Ellen.

As soon as Mrs. Otis was busy writing sentences on the board, Jessica passed Lila a note. It read, THAT WAS GREAT!

Lila read the note. She smiled and nodded at Jessica. Lila passed the note to Ellen, who wrote something on the paper. The note started its way back to Jessica.

When Jessica got the note, she saw that Ellen had written, CAROLINE IS A BIG BABY. AND A FINK.

Jessica started to write a reply, but Lila poked her in the side. She looked up and saw Mrs. Otis walk up her aisle. Jessica slipped the note under her leg. She started to copy the sentences off the board. She let out her breath as Mrs. Otis walked by her desk.

The teacher stopped next to Todd's desk. Jessica peeked behind her. Todd hadn't noticed that Mrs. Otis was standing over him. He was concentrating on writing something in his notebook. Jessica raised her eyebrows at Elizabeth.

"Are you copying Ken's homework, Todd?" Mrs. Otis asked.

Todd jumped about a foot out of his seat. "No," he said, trying to hide the papers on his desk.

Mrs. Otis put out her hand. "I'll take those."

Todd gave her the papers. He looked miserable. Mrs. Otis didn't mind if the students in her class helped each other. But copying was not allowed. Mrs. Otis wanted each person to do his or her own work.

"Copying someone else's answers is no way to learn." Mrs. Otis was speaking softly, but Jessica could hear every word. Jessica knew Elizabeth could hear, too. "Especially when you are having trouble in math."

"But I got a B on my last test," Todd said.

Jessica shook her head. She couldn't believe Todd was bragging to Mrs. Otis about a grade he got by cheating.

"I know that," Mrs. Otis said. "It was a big improvement over your last

test grade. I also noticed that you and Ken missed the same problems on the fractions test. You had the same answers on the problems you got wrong, too. Is there something you boys want to tell me?" She looked from Todd to Ken.

There was a long pause.

"Todd, did you cheat on the test?" Mrs. Otis asked.

"Yes," Todd whispered.

"Ken, did you help him?"

"I guess," Ken told her.

"Todd, I want you to take the test again tomorrow after school," Mrs. Otis said. "That will give you time to study."

"OK," Todd said quietly.

"In the meantime both of you come up to my desk," Mrs. Otis said. "I'm going to write a note explaining what happened. You can take it to Mrs. Armstrong's office. She'll give you your punishment."

Mrs. Otis went back down the aisle. Ken and Todd were right behind her. The boys were dragging their feet. Jessica thought she heard Todd sniffle. Jessica knew she would cry if Mrs. Otis caught her cheating.

"Poor Todd," Elizabeth whispered to Jessica.

Jessica nodded. Mrs. Otis hardly ever sent anyone to the principal's office. But cheating was serious. Todd was sure to get in a lot of trouble. Ken would be in trouble, too. He was going to be mad at Todd for that.

CHAPTER 9

Tattletales

Elizabeth couldn't concentrate on her math problems. Ken and Todd had been gone for almost twenty minutes. Elizabeth could only think about what was going on in Mrs. Armstrong's office.

Finally the classroom door opened. Todd and Ken came in. Elizabeth tried to catch Todd's eye, but he looked away.

"I have to go down the hall for a few minutes," Mrs. Otis told the class. "Please behave yourselves while I'm gone."

As soon as Mrs. Otis was out the

door, Elizabeth twisted around so she was facing Todd. "What happened?"

Todd looked angry. "What happened?" he repeated. "You told on us. That's what happened!"

Elizabeth's eyes were wide. "I did not!"

"Don't try and act innocent," Todd said. He lowered his voice. "You were the only one who knew I cheated."

"I didn't tell," Elizabeth said. "I swear."

Todd rolled his eyes. "I bet. From now on, I don't want to talk to you."

Elizabeth turned back around. She tried to understand how Mrs. Otis had found out. She hadn't told the teacher. Ken hadn't told her. And Todd certainly hadn't told her. That left only one person.

Elizabeth leaned over to her sister. "I can't believe you told."

"What do you mean?" Jessica asked.

"You told Mrs. Otis that Todd cheated," Elizabeth said.

Jessica looked surprised. "I did not!"

"Who else would have?" Elizabeth yelled. "Now I'm not talking to you."

Jessica slumped down in her seat. After a few minutes, she wrote a note and passed it to Lila. Lila read the note and passed it to Ellen. Ellen read it. Both girls looked angry.

Lila, Jessica, and Ellen got up and marched over to Caroline's desk. The three girls stood in front of Caroline with their arms folded across their chests.

"What do you want?" Caroline asked.

"You're a tattletale," Jessica said to Caroline.

Caroline's face turned red. "I am not!"

"Are too!" Lila said.

"You've been tattling on us all week, so

you must be the one who told on Todd. You were right there when Elizabeth told me about it," Jessica said. "I saw you."

"So we're never going to talk to you again," Ellen said.

Caroline started to cry. Jessica didn't care.

As Jessica, Lila, and Ellen sat down again, Mrs. Otis came back into the room. That's when Caroline let out a huge sob.

"What's wrong now, Caroline?" Mrs. Otis asked her. "Are you crying?"

Caroline nodded without a word.

Mrs. Otis looked out over the class. "I see a lot of unhappy faces in here. What happened? Ken, why are you frowning?"

"Because I'm in trouble," Ken said. "And it's all Todd's fault."

"We only got in trouble because

Elizabeth told on us," Todd said.

"I did not tell!" Elizabeth yelled. "Jessica did."

"Nuh-uh," Jessica said. "Caroline did."

Mrs. Otis shook her head. "For your information, nobody told on anyone. Ken and Todd had the exact same problems wrong on their tests. Plus, Todd's work improved a little too much a little too fast." She looked directly at Todd and Ken. "I've been watching the two of you for days, and I caught you red-handed. You don't get to be a teacher by being stupid, you know."

Mrs. Otis looked at all the embarrassed faces. She gave the class a reading assignment. During the quiet that followed, everyone had plenty of time to think.

CHAPTER 10

Soccer Tickets

Jessica took a bite of her sandwich. It was tuna fish, her favorite, but Jessica was too angry to enjoy it.

Elizabeth unwrapped her own identical sandwich. She put it down without taking a bite. "I'm sorry I called you a tattletale," she said.

Jessica frowned. "I never tell on anyone."

"I know," Elizabeth said. "I said I was sorry."

"OK," Jessica said.

"Friends?" Elizabeth asked.

"Friends," Jessica agreed.

Todd and Ken approached the girls' table. The boys looked as if they had already made up. "I'm sorry, Elizabeth," Todd whispered, looking at his feet. "You aren't a tattletale. And you were right. Cheating is wrong."

Elizabeth smiled. "I forgive you."

Todd looked up. "Really? That's great!"

The boys sat down and started to eat their lunches. Soon Elizabeth, Ken, and Todd were talking and laughing. But Jessica didn't join in. Something was bothering her. There was something she had to do.

Jessica went to find Lila and Ellen, who were on the lunch line. The three girls walked over to where Caroline was eating.

"We're sorry," Jessica told Caroline.

"You should be!" Caroline burst out.

"I know," Jessica said. "We are." She turned to look at Lila and Ellen. "Right?"

"Right," Lila mumbled.

"Yeah," Ellen said softly.

Caroline nodded. "Thanks a lot."

"That doesn't mean we're sorry for scaring you with the frog. You did tell on us about our jokes," Lila said.

"Next time we won't tell you any secrets," Jessica added.

The three girls ran back to their table. Jessica was happy everyone was friends again. She didn't expect to hear anything more about cheating for a long, long time. But as soon as class started again after lunch, Todd raised his hand.

"Um, Mrs. Otis . . . I have to tell you something," Todd said.

"What is it?" Mrs. Otis asked.

"I—I cheated during the spelling bee." Todd looked down at his desk.

"I thought so, but I wasn't sure about that," Mrs. Otis said. "Thank you for telling us, Todd. Admitting that you did something wrong takes a lot of courage. Now I'm going to let you decide what would be the right thing to do with the soccer tickets."

Todd thought for a minute. "I guess I'll give them to Jessica. She came in second. If I hadn't cheated, she would have won."

It was Jessica's turn to make an announcement. "I only like to watch soccer when Elizabeth is playing," she said. "So I'm going to give the tickets to Liz. I know she wants them more than I do."

Elizabeth beamed. "Thanks, Jessica.

But there are three tickets. One for me, one for Dad, and one for you."

Jessica made a face. "No, thanks."

"I'll go," Eva called out.

Elizabeth laughed. "It's a deal."

"Hurray!" Eva yelled.

Eva ran up to Jessica and Elizabeth the next day before school started. "Did you get them?" she asked Elizabeth eagerly.

Todd was supposed to bring the soccer tickets to school that day and give them to Elizabeth.

"Not yet," Elizabeth said. "Todd isn't here yet."

"I hope he's not absent," Eva said.

"Me too," Jessica said. The game wasn't for a few days. But she knew how excited Elizabeth was. It was all she had talked about since yesterday.

"There's Todd," Eva said. "Come on!"

The three girls hurried over to him. As they approached, Todd started shaking his head.

"What's the matter?" Eva demanded.

"The tickets are gone," Todd said.

"What?" Jessica gasped.

"My dad gave them away," Todd said, looking miserable. "I'm sorry."

Eva and Elizabeth exchanged looks.

"Don't worry, Todd," Elizabeth choked out. "It's—it's not a big deal."

"What do you mean, it's not a big deal?" Jessica shouted.

"Really, Jess, I'll get over it. There'll be other games."

"Yeah," Eva mumbled. "We can read about it in the paper—even though that's not the same as being there."

"Got you!" Todd shouted.

71

Elizabeth's and Eva's mouths dropped open.

Todd pulled the tickets out of his pocket. He was grinning. "You should have seen your faces! That was great. It was even better than the jokes you've been playing all week, Jessica."

Elizabeth grabbed the tickets. "Very funny!"

"It's not April Fools' Day yet, you know," Eva told Todd.

"I'm just practicing," Todd said. "It's coming up."

"You're just jealous," Jessica told Todd.

"Yeah. If you had studied, you would be going to the game. Instead, you're going to be serving detention for a week," Elizabeth said.

"That's why you'd better enjoy these tickets," Todd said. "Next time, I *am* going to study!"

"You'd better watch out on April Fools' Day," Jessica told Todd. "We're going to get you back."

Elizabeth smiled at her sister. "I can hardly wait."

Todd laughed. "Don't be so sure. I might get you again."

Who will think up the best April Fools' joke? Find out in Sweet Valley Kids #48, Lila's April Fool.

SIGN UP FOR THE SWEET VALLEY HIGH® FAN CLUB!

Hey, girls! Get all the gossip on Sweet Valley High's® most popular teenagers when you join our fantastic Fan Club! As a member, you'll get all of this really cool stuff:

- Membership Card with your own personal Fan Club ID number
- A Sweet Valley High® Secret Treasure Box
- Sweet Valley High® Stationery
- Official Fan Club Pencil (for secret note writing!)
- Three Bookmarks
- A "Members Only" Door Hanger
- Two Skeins of J. & P. Coats® Embroidery Floss with flower barrette instruction leaflet
- Two editions of *The Oracle* newsletter
- Plus exclusive Sweet Valley High® product offers, special savings, contests, and much more!

Be the first to find out what Jessica & Elizabeth Wakefield are up to by joining the Sweet Valley High® Fan Club for the one-year membership fee of only $6.25 each for U.S. residents, $8.25 for Canadian residents (U.S. currency). Includes shipping & handling.

Send a check or money order (do not send cash) made payable to "Sweet Valley High® Fan Club" along with this form to:

SWEET VALLEY HIGH® FAN CLUB, BOX 3919-B, SCHAUMBURG, IL 60168-3919

NAME __Lindsay Ica__
(Please print clearly)

ADDRESS __1091 Bright Stream Way__

CITY __Rochester__   STATE __NY__ ZIP __14580__
(Required)

AGE __7__   BIRTHDAY __7__ / __11__ / __86__

THE UNICORN CLUB

HANG WITH THE COOLEST KIDS AROUND!

Jessica and Elizabeth Wakefield are just two of the terrific members of The Unicorn Club you've met in *Sweet Valley Twins and Friends*. Now get to know some of their friends even better! Share in their exciting adventures with this great new series. Join The Unicorn Club and become a part of the friendship and fun!

THE UNICORN CLUB

FRANCINE PASCAL

THE UNICORN CLUB

A Sensational NEW Sweet Valley Series!

THE UNICORN CLUB

② MARIA'S MOVIE COMEBACK